*Julián Ayesta*

*Helena or The Sea in Summer*

Translated and with an introduction by
Margaret Jull Costa

Dedalus

Dedalus would like to thank The General Direction for Books, Archives and Librar-
ies of The Spanish Ministry of Culture for its support in publishing this book.

Published in the UK by Dedalus Limited,
24–26 St Judith's Lane, Sawtry, Cambs, PE28 5XE
email: info@dedalusbooks.com
www.dedalusbooks.com

ISBN 978 1 903517 59 8

Dedalus is distributed in the USA by SCB Distributors,
15608 South New Century Drive, Gardena, CA 90248
email: info@scbdistributors.com    web: www.scbdistributors.com

Dedalus is distributed in Australia by Peribo Pty Ltd,
58 Beaumont Road, Mount Kuring-gai, N.S.W. 2080
email: info@peribo.com.au

Dedalus is distributed in Canada by Disticor Direct-Book Division
695, Westney Road South, Suite 14, Ajax, Ontario, LI6 6M9
email: ndalton@disticor.com    web, www.disticordirect.com

First published in Spain in 1952
*First published by Dedalus in 2008*

*Helena o el mar del verano copyright © 1952, 1974, 1987, 2000 the heirs of Julián Ayesta*
*Copyright © 1987, 2000 Acantilado (Quaderns Crema S.A.)*
*Translation copyright © Margaret Jull Costa 2008*

The right of the heirs of Julián Ayesta to be identified as the copyright holders of this
work and Margaret Jull Costa to be identified as the translator of this work has been
asserted by them accordance with the Copyright, Designs and Patent Act, 1988

Printed in Finland by WS Bookwell
Typeset by RefineCatch Limited, Bungay, Suffolk

A C.I.P. listing for this book is available on request.

Dedalus Euro Shorts
General Editor: Mike Mitchell

# Helena or
# The Sea in Summer

## THE TRANSLATOR

Margaret Jull Costa has been a literary translator for over twenty years and has translated many novels and short stories by Portuguese, Spanish and Latin American writers. She was joint-winner of the 1992 Portuguese Translation Prize for *The Book of Disquiet* by Fernando Pessoa, won the translator's portion of the 1997 International IMPAC Dublin Literary Award for *A Heart So White* by Javier Marías, the 2000 Weidenfeld Translation Prize for José Saramago's *All the Names*, and the 2006 Valle-Inclán Prize for *Your Face Tomorrow: Fever and Spear* by Javier Marías.

## TRANSLATOR'S ACKNOWLEDGEMENTS

I would, as always, like to thank Annella McDermott and Ben Sherriff for all their help and advice. I am indebted, too, for much of the biographical information about Julián Ayesta, to Antonio Pau's excellent introduction to Ayesta's *Cuentos* (Pre-Textos, 2001) and to Ayesta's own writings published in *Dibujos y poemas* (ed. Antonio Pau, Editorial Trotta, 2003).

# CONTENTS

*In you I desired the green grass, the cool breeze,*
*The white lily and the red rose,*
*And the sweet spring.*

Garcilaso de la Vega, *First Eclogue*


*But far away are the distant days*
*when love seemed one with radiant nature,*
*and when a happy, potent noontide*
*filled the heart and laid a world at one's feet.*

Vicente Aleixandre, 'Power of the night' from
*Sombra del Paraíso* (*Shadow of Paradise*)

# INTRODUCTION

Julián Ayesta (1919–1996) was born in Gijón, the largest city in the northern Spanish province of Asturias. His family were reasonably wealthy. His father was a lawyer, a Republican member of parliament and editor of two local newspapers. At the age of fifteen, despite his father's allegiance to the Republic, Ayesta joined the Falange, the Fascist movement founded by José Antonio Primo de Rivera. He did so, he wrote, because 'it was the fashionable thing to do'. When Civil War broke out in 1936, Ayesta volunteered to fight on the side of the Nationalists. He was captured, briefly imprisoned, then freed to return to the front where he fought until the end of the war in 1939. He soon became disillusioned with the Nationalist victory, however, and, after studying at the university of Madrid, he opted to become a diplomat and subsequently spent large periods of his adult life abroad. Alongside his diplomatic duties, he wrote articles, poems, short stories and plays. On visits to Spain, he was a regular at the famous literary *tertulia* (discussion group) at Café Gijón and knew and was known by all the writers of his generation. He loathed the bitter divisions that remained after the Civil War and the way that these divisions were fomented and encouraged by the Franco regime. In 1946, he wrote:

Nothing is lost if we take each other's hand.
Loyally, man to man.
If we take each other's hand
despite all the subcommittees and
     commissions
despite all the congresses, plenary meetings
     and mediations;
despite the foreigners who had no part in
     our struggle.
If we take each other's hand man to man
despite the politicians,

despite all those who never got involved,
    despite the dispassionate bystanders,
    the sceptics and the cowards.
If we take each other's hand as Spaniard to
    Spaniard. . .

In 1952, he published *Helena o el mar en verano* to great critical acclaim. In 1956, his involvement in drawing up a manifesto for the nascent student union movement in his old university in Madrid got him despatched to Beirut, but when he came back to Madrid in 1968, he immediately became a contributor to the newspaper *SP*, whose aim was 'to be the equivalent of a real national conscience: objective, balanced, progressive and removed from any kind of localism, dogmatism, or submission to particular groups or political parties'. The newspaper lasted only two years. The front-page articles that Ayesta wrote for *SP* were considered so outspoken that, to protect him, they were signed only with a number – 586.847 – the number on his identity card. In his final article (just before *SP* was closed down), he denounced the alleged suicide of a student in police custody and the government's use of the student's diaries to besmirch his name. He came very close to losing his job in the diplomatic service. Instead, he was sent to Sudan on a hardship mission - to set up a Spanish embassy in Khartoum. Despite the heat and the epidemics and the mosquitos, he continued to write critical articles in one of the few Spanish newspapers to remain politically independent, *Sábado Gráfico*, until that too was closed down by the censor.

Ayesta spent four long, uncomfortable years in Khartoum, and his time there ended abruptly in 1973 when a group belonging to the Al-Fatah movement burst into an embassy reception and kidnapped several diplomats, killing two United States ambassadors and one Belgian ambassador. Since Spain was the only country involved that did not, at the time, recognise Israel, Ayesta became the chief mediator between kidnappers and negotiators, and, in the end, the remaining hostages were all released unharmed. Paradoxically, having been posted to Khartoum as a punishment, he was now summoned to Madrid where he was received with great pomp and ceremony, awarded the

Grand Cross of Civil Merit and given the best diplomatic posting imaginable: Consul General in Amsterdam. He continued to work and travel and write: articles, another novel (never finished and never published), and grim, often surreal plays in which the civil war was always there in the background. Few of these plays ever got past the censor.

However, in 1980, he again returned to Madrid, this time to a Spain undergoing rapid change after Franco's death in 1975 and to a Spain enjoying absolute freedom of the press. He immediately resumed his collaboration with *Sábado Gráfico*. After two further postings to Alexandria and Belgrade, he was forced to retire early and went back to Gijón, to the house where he had been born and where he died in 1996 of cancer.

Apart from the incomplete and unpublished *Cena ligera con final feliz* [*A Light Supper with a Happy Ending*], *Helena* was Ayesta's only novel and it is the work for which he is best remembered. The stories that make up *Helena* had been written and published separately over the previous ten years, and he only brought them together as a 'novel' later. He said that he had wanted to create 'a kind of song' and had written the stories:

> . . .with the deliberate aim of exalting all that is eternally valuable, noble and beautiful about life. It is a Mediterranean reaction against the kind of angst-ridden pseudo-existentialism that invents a life far removed from the human life that I have invented in Helena.

On publication, the book was warmly reviewed and it has been reprinted several times over the years. Critics praised the author's evoca-tion of innocence and joy, and when one considers what a very grim, joyless place post-Civil War Spain was, it is hard not to experience *Helena* as a deeply subversive book. Most of the novels written at the time were rural or urban dramas in the mould of social realism, haunted (as, indeed, were Ayesta's plays) by the ghosts of the recent past. What Ayesta evokes is not only first love and childhood, but also a lost and irrecoverable paradise; and what stands, unnamed, between the writer/reader and that paradise is the terrible, brutal civil war that continued in the bitter aftermath of Francoism. The book seems to be saying in the most joyous and passionate terms possible: This is what we have lost.

The childhood setting and the innocent voice of the narrator allow Ayesta to smuggle in glimpses of a very different reality – the kindly Republican and atheist, Don Robustiano, whom the boys cannot bring themselves to insult to his face; the gruesome acts of violence (not far removed from the atrocities perpetrated by both sides in the Spanish Civil War) which he imagines committing in defence of the Virgin; the man at the cider bar sidling up to his father and making some offensive remark; the song: 'If your good father was here...' (so many good fathers were not); the ghostly, nightmarish figures thought to inhabit the eucalyptus woods. Safe in this pre-war haven and under the guise of childish humour, anarchic Uncle Arturo is free to poke fun at the devout, priggish Ladies – particularly Aunt Honorina – and the narrator can gleefully

17

imagine spitting at 'the ladies in black, wearing gold-rimmed spectacles' whom he passes in the street; the recalcitrant student of Classics can take pleasure in the sound of Virgil's Latin and his celebration of nature, in implicit contrast to the dead Latin of the Catholic Mass and the stifling, guilt-ridden world described in 'God's joy'.

The language Ayesta uses is itself rebellious, full of apparent redundancies – a vast silent silence; metaphors and similes that breathe life into the inanimate – the sun snoring above the apple trees, colours as sharp as knives; and (in the earlier sections) the use of a child's voice as narrator – all those concatenated sentences: And. . . And. . . And. . . – all those seemingly random thoughts and responses. The child's view of the world – all smells and colours and noises – gives the prose a rare vital freshness.

Then there is Helena herself, who is the very embodiment of freedom. She it is who calls a halt to the 'Battle of Verdun'. She is the pagan goddess of the woods and the sea. In the final section, 'Afternoon and twilight', she is everything that the younger narrator of 'God's joy' was told by the priests was wrong and sinful – she is sexual and sensual and open and loving; they even kiss away the blood from the scratches inflicted by the brambles, tasting each other's blood, half-conscious that what they are doing is a sin – a secret rite. In the dream sequence – a plunge into the Ancient World – where even the writing follows a curious archaic syntax, sex is not a sin but a celebration. And the sheer physical pleasure of flinging themselves into the 'cold, white, bubbling wave[s], so beautiful, so delicious, so furiously joyful that it made one mad with happiness' is a gauntlet flung in the face of the prim, grey, vengeful place that Spain had become under Franco.

Ayesta himself struggled to know what term to use to describe *Helena*: Autobiography? Poem? A novel with all the non-essential chapters omitted? A kind of pointillist novel? He concluded: 'Let's not call it anything.' Perhaps the best description is his own, quoted earlier: 'a kind of song. . .exalting all that is eternally valuable, noble and beautiful about life' – what better weapon to use against fascism and repression and fear.

# I

# SUMMER

1

## LUNCH IN THE GARDEN

The cherry jam shone bright red amongst the black and yellow wasps, and the wind stirred the branches of the oak trees, and spots of sunlight raced over the moss, over the soft, damp grass and over the faces of the guests and of the Men and Women, who were all smoking and laughing. And the dessert spoons and the blue glasses set out for the Marie Brizard liqueur, they shone too. And the polka-dots of light – the large ones chasing the smaller ones – scurried over the table-cloth which was all covered with purple wine stains and breadcrumbs. There was a bullfight that afternoon, and the men had shiny faces, cheeks and noses. The coffee shone too, black amongst the cigar ash in the saucer. And the men all wore lopsided grins because they had a cigar

in their mouth and talked and laughed like toothless old crocks, poking out tongues bright with
spit as they blew out clouds of blue smoke. And it
was really lovely to see how the colour of the
smoke changed as the sun caught it. And because
it was Assumption Day, we children had been to
throw rose petals at the Virgin, and there had
been bagpipes and rockets and violins and the
sound of singing from inside the church. And
everything smelled of incense and flowers and
doughnuts and sweet fritters and of the cider
being drunk by the men in the Campo de la
Iglesia and of new clothes. And when we ran over
to the cars, everything smelled of petrol, and the
priests (except you don't call them 'priests' you
call them 'holy fathers') who had led the sung
mass came home with us for lunch. And before
we sat down to lunch they pinched our cheeks
and asked us our names and if we knew which
day was our saint's day and whether our saint
was a Holy Confessor or a Holy Bishop or a Holy
Virgin or a Holy Hermit (what *is* a hermit?) and
if we knew that the pagans used to throw these
people to the lions in the circus in Rome. And the

24

holy fathers smelled very delicate, very different from the other grown-ups because they were Ministers of God, and they protested when everyone urged them to serve themselves first and said: 'No, no, I wouldn't hear of it', and Uncle Arturo said: 'It's not every day we have a mitre in the house.' (What's a mitre? 'Children, be quiet.') And everyone laughed and Don José started talking and stammering: 'P-please, r-really. . .', but everyone carried on laughing and the children did too, covering their faces with their napkins. And then Don José got up to say grace and we all prayed:

> *Jesus Christ, King of Life,*
> *He who was born in a humble stable,*
> *Bless the food upon this table,*
> *Lord of All, Amen.*

We had only got as far as 'stable', when grandma lost her teeth, and they fell in the fingerbowl, spattering the tablecloth with water, and we all laughed, even Don José. And so we had to start again:

25

*Jesus Christ, King of Life,*
*He who was born in a humble stable,*
*Bless the food upon this table,*
*Lord of All, Amen.*

And Uncle Arturo always said: 'Is there some other Jesus Christ who wasn't born in a stable?' and Aunt Honorina would say: 'Uh oh, he's gone all Voltairean on us,' and the holy fathers would laugh, and then each group would go their different ways: the women indoors to get dressed up for the bullfight, the children to the pond to continue the Great Naval Battle of Lepanto, and the men to their seats under the oak trees, where they drank more coffee and liqueurs and, now and then, roared with laughter, probably at some joke or other. Then, suddenly, the men leapt to their feet because Don José's armchair had broken and he'd fallen backwards and banged his head on a nail that we children had hammered into the trunk of an oak tree all overgrown with ivy. And it was so odd, too horrible to think about really, to see a priest bleeding, his whole neck covered in very bright, very red blood and a red, red thread of

26

blood running down the back of his black cassock. And it was so dreadful and so sinful that we children were afraid to look because we didn't think priests had any blood in them, only a soul and some bones. And while all the grown-ups were rushing around screaming and bringing jugs of water and medicines and bandages and cotton wool, we went into the coachhouse and hid in the trap, which smelled really nice, of old things, and which was left there in the dark because it hadn't been used for ages and we weren't supposed to get in it because the last horse that had been hitched to it had died of tetanus.

## 2

## AT THE BEACH

In the late afternoons, the beach was full of orange sun and there were lots of white clouds and everything smelled of potato and onion omelette.

And there were crabs that hid among the rocks, and we children were put in charge of burying the bottles of cider in the damp sand to keep them cool.

And everyone said: 'What a glorious afternoon', and the young couples sat apart from the rest of us, and when it began to grow dark and everything was lilac and purple, they would sit very silently with their faces pressed close, as if they were in confession.

But the best part was the late afternoon swim, when the sun was going down and was huge and kept getting redder and redder, and the sea was first green, then a darker green, then blue, then indigo, and then almost black. And the water was *so* warm, and there were shoals of tiny fishes swimming in and out of the reddish seaweed.

And it was fun diving down and pinching the women on their legs to make them squeal. And then Papa and Uncle Arturo and Aunt Josefina's husband would lift us up onto their shoulders and let us dive into the water from there. And then two of them would grab one of us and hurl us through the air, saying: 'In he goes, squirming like a cat!' and the women, bottoms bulging in their ante-diluvian costumes, would say: 'Stop messing around with the kids.' And then the men would say to us: 'Come on, let's give 'em a fright' and we would chase Mama and our aunts and the other ladies and they would scuttle screaming out of the water and up the beach until we caught them and dragged them back, captive, to the shore, and there they would sit on the sand, terrified, and Aunt Honorina, close to tears, would say to her husband: 'No, please, Arturín, no.' And we kids would kill ourselves laughing when she called Uncle Arturo 'Arturín', and for at least an hour afterwards, until we got tired of it, we would all call him 'Arturín'. But then we would join hands (the women's hands would be shaking) and run into the water together and plunge in, not the women though, they would sit down where the water was only about two inches deep, laughing like a lot of broody hens. And stupid Albertito would always open his mouth and gulp down lots of water and sand and then vomit it up and be left with a bitter burning sensation inside.

And it was so funny to see Aunt Josefina's legs under the water, they seemed to swell and shrink and were the same disgusting greenish white as a toad's belly.

And there was an older girl who had just arrived from Madrid, very pretty and very tanned, with really big eyes and smelling of a perfume that made you feel all funny.

And she had a very clear, sad sort of voice and she used to say to us boys: 'Which one of you is brave enough to swim with me out to the Camel,' but no one ever dared, not Papa, not Uncle Arturo, not Aunt Josefina's husband, not us, and then she would swim all alone out to the Camel,

31

which was so far off you could hardly see it, and she didn't care if the sea was rough or if it was one of those grey days when you felt afraid even to go in the water. And she swam wearing the bracelets that she always wore, and we would watch as one arm then the other emerged shining and wet, the bracelets glinting in the sun, and because she was swimming crawl, her feet left behind them a wake of foam.

And there was a bald German gentleman, who wore white bathing trunks and always had two dogs with him, and his skin was burned red, almost black, from spending all day in the sun, fishing and reading the newspaper, with a white towel over his shoulders. And we would have our afternoon snack on the beach, and for the children there were the lunchtime leftovers, tuna, omelette and cutlets fried in breadcrumbs, and for dessert we had a choice of oranges, apples, pears, grapes, cherries or peaches. And there were bananas too, and we used to have fun squeezing them at one end so that the flesh popped out the other and then showing them to the grown-ups; it always made the men laugh, though we never knew why.

And the slices of omelette and the cutlets were all gritty with sand, and the little girls' wet hair stuck to their faces, and their eyes shone, and they would scream and leap about amongst the dogs, who would leap about too and bark and run to fetch the bits of dry seaweed that were thrown for them, and then the girls would give them any scraps that were left over, and there was always loads: omelette, cutlets, tuna, and the dogs would lick the empty sardine tins until the tins shone like mirrors, and King would even eat the peel from the fruit, although he was the only dog that did.

And because the men said that we mustn't leave a scrap of paper or any rubbish on the beach, 'because we had to set a good example', we would pile up the cardboard trays and the bits of greasy paper and the peel and set fire to it all and then bury the ashes along with the cans that wouldn't burn in the fire.

And then we would go and get dressed behind the rocks. And the sand was really cold, and a cold wind came whipping through, making us shiver because, by then, it was growing dark.

And then everyone – apart from the ladies –

would pick up a bag and we would set off home. And we would walk along singing and picking blackberries, which were still warm from the sun.

And our backs were all sticky and stinging, and a great fat moon would be coming up.

And the frogs and the toads would be singing too.

And everything smelled of thyme.

And then we would have to go past the cider-houses and the bars, which were full of men drinking and playing skittles and pitch-and-toss.

And it was good to hear the sound of wood on wood or the clink of metal on metal.

And there was a man who sang really well, and Papa said why didn't we sit down at one of the tables and rest a while, and he ordered cider for everyone, including the children, and it tickled and bubbled as it went down.

And that was when the stars would come out.

And from time to time, you'd notice a very dark patch of sea, so dark that just the thought of swimming there all alone made you feel afraid.

And Papa and Uncle Arturo asked Aunt Josefina to sing 'I've got three little goats', but she turned bright red and said how could she possibly sing in front of all those people, and everyone laughed.

And suddenly a man came over, stinking of wine, and he clapped my father on the back and said something I couldn't hear.

And Papa gave him a nasty look, then immediately paid the bill, and we left.

You could hear music coming from a Sunday dance somewhere.

And by the time we reached Gijón, we were all very quiet, almost sad.

And the lights in the streets were sad too.

And on the beach, you could see the Yachting Club decorated with coloured lights.

And there were lots of people in the street, and a band marched past, playing.

And cars with white wheels went by.

And the streets were all newly washed and shining and black.

And everything smelled of hot tyres and cologne and sea.

All because the Prince of Asturias was visiting Gijón.

3

## ONE NIGHT

Every year it was the same; it was the night of the holidays when we always had the most fun.

Our house wasn't quite ready yet, and so we children were sleeping at Uncle Arturo and Aunt Honorina's house.

I slept on a divan bed in the same room as Alberto and José (whom we called the Big Baby because up until he was eight years old or more, his mother used to go chasing him round the garden with a baby's bottle in her hand, shouting: 'Come here, Pepín, come here, your milk's getting cold!') and the girls slept in the other room.

Between the two bedrooms there was a communicating door, which was kept closed.

It was a very shiny white door which, for some

reason, was very pleasing to look at, with its red wooden doorknob, shaped like a ball.

This doorknob just above my head was a source of great anxiety to Aunt Honorina, who used to say:

'I knew a gentleman in Gijón who broke his neck on something just like that.'

She knew everyone and anyone who had died a strange death: hundreds and thousands of gentlemen-from-Gijón and ladies-from-Gijón who had been beheaded by lift doors or electro-cuted when ringing the bell for the servants while still in the bath or who had died of pneumonia because they'd refused to put on a sweater after playing football.

But that was always 'a-long-long-time-ago' and I'll-tell-you-about-it-properly-another-day' and, besides, they were grown-ups, not little boys like you.

But now Aunt Honorina was saying goodnight to us from the door.

The light from the staircase was on; Aunt Honorina's shadow was walking across the blu-ish ceiling of the bedroom and, against the light, her head had a golden halo round it, like a saint's.

'Go to sleep now,' she said.

She was just about to leave when we heard the toilet flush and the door open.

A new light entered the room and my aunt's shadow on the ceiling became first two and then one again.

'Frivolous' Uncle Arturo was approaching down the corridor, singing softly to himself, and in the next room, the girls started screaming because they knew Uncle Arturo would come creeping in on his haunches, saying: 'What news, my distinguished young ladies?' in the falsetto voice of a dwarf, just to scare them.

'Oh, Arturo, really, don't get them all ex-cited now,' – and it was so funny to hear the way she said 'ex-cited' – 'you're worse than the boys, you are,' said my aunt.

But it was too late; the most horrendous racket was coming from the girls' room.

Aunt Honorina ran off in the direction of the tumult, crying out in her shrill voice, saying what she always said:

'Oh, dear God, don't scream like that! I thought something terrible had happened. Just feel how my heart's pounding. You'll be the death of me one day!'

But she didn't die, no one ever felt her heart, and nothing terrible happened. It was just that Aunt Honorina was an idiot.

There were a lot of shadows on the ceiling now, passing each other and disappearing.

On the landing, Aunt Honorina was saying that frights like that could damage a child's heart and she started telling Uncle Arturo the story of the only child of the Marquis and Marchioness of something or other, whom she'd met when she went to Rome to see the Pope and visited the Scala in Milan on the way back, and the Marquis and Marchioness – such a coincidence – were in the seats next to theirs, not that she knew who they were, of course, because I'm not the sort who thinks that knowing people of the nobility is anything special, because what we need in this country aren't foolish aristocrats, but good Catholics and good Spaniards, anyway, where was I, ah yes, anyway, they must have heard us speaking Spanish, because they turned round and said: 'Are you Spanish?' and we got talking and they were such nice people, no airs or graces, especially not her, such a nice woman, I mean, he was nice too, of course, a really decent man, and I just wish all those upper-class types could be more like him, then you wouldn't get the kind of goings-on you do now, he took communion every day and gave alms most generously, not that he drew attention to it, mind, he was always most discreet, anyway, it's men like him who'll be the saviours of Spain, not that there are many of them around, and, to be perfectly frank, between you and me, I think what's happening now is a punishment from God; anyway, where was I, ah, yes, the poor things had a daughter with a very delicate heart and all because of a nursemaid they'd employed, I mean, they're such oafs these women; I knew one who used to turn on the gas to get the child to sleep, and it's just as well they caught her at it one night because you can imagine what might have happened, and she wasn't a bad person, just ignorant, like most of the lower orders, and now, of course, it's even

41

worse because it's almost impossible to even *find* a nursemaid, etc. etc.

Finally, the supper gong sounded below, and they went downstairs, leaving us children alone on the floor above.

That was when the expedition began. Or, rather, The Expedition, because it was very important indeed.

It could only happen on that one night of the year: the great Battle of Verdun, a cruel and mysterious battle.

It involved arming ourselves with pillows and bundling our way into the girls' room, although, of course, they might have already heard us coming down the corridor (both our bedrooms led off it, theirs and ours) and gone to hide behind the shutters with their own pillows at the ready, perhaps clutching full glasses of water from the bedside table and simultaneously trying to hold in their laughter and hold up their pyjama bottoms, which kept coming untied.

And it was so exciting, especially the stealthy advance down the corridor, which was bright with moonlight and full of the sound of croaking frogs and whistling toads and the whisper of the sea far off, and you could see the car headlights as they crossed the bridge, and it made you feel like running out stark naked into the night, breathing hard, going nowhere.

And it was so exciting, too, sneaking into the bedroom if the girls weren't ready (as happened the summer before last) and, in the moonlight, getting hold of the sheets and pulling them off the bed and then, when the girls tried to get up, hitting them round the head with a pillow and then taking all the bedclothes so that they couldn't protect themselves with the blankets and escaping down the corridor when they turned on us, fierce as cornered jackals, absolutely fuming, and came after us, in full chase, clutching their pillows and finally catching up with us, which was when the fighting became hand-to-hand combat, with Helena's hair tickling my face and me grabbing her and, with just a look, trying to cow her into begging for mercy and her refusing and me hearing her say angrily: 'Brute, animal, beast, idiot,' and then bursting into tears in a way that was quite different from normal, very sad, but filled with something that was neither sorrow nor joy, an odd sound that made me feel like crying too, very quietly, in some hidden place where no one would hear me, and to cry and cry for the rest of my life, glad to be crying and crying.

Alberto slowly sat up in bed and said 'psst'. José and I answered him and the three of us tiptoed towards the corridor, each carrying a white pillow.

A vast silent silence, colder than in Orbelkismoff Grandsen Lewisky's grotto after his daughter, Princess Alda, had drowned in the sad lake at evening and the melancholy voice of Julia called and called from the tops of the Rocky Mountains, all hope almost gone; a silence ripe for repeating 'quacumque, quacumque, quacumque' in some distant forest, as if in a cathedral of the dead somewhere on the high, cold, solitary table-lands of Tibet.

Alberto put his head round the door of the girls' bedroom, then made a gesture meaning 'all quiet, safe to advance', and we crept in.

The girls were sleeping peacefully like pale-blue velvet kittens. I went over to Helena's bed.

She gave off a warm smell, rather like a nest with baby birds in it. She was sleeping with her face buried in the pillow, her long, fair hair caught back behind her. She was breathing very slowly, so gently that I felt guilty about pulling the sheets off her bed in order to begin the battle. But then Alberto looked at me and I closed my eyes and tugged at the bedspread, trembling with remorse. I hardly knew what I was doing.

Helena woke with a scream, and the pillow-fight commenced. The bedside lamp leapt off the dressing-table and crashed against the wall opposite, making a sharp, unpleasant sound.

'The Battle of Verdun, the Battle of Verdun!' shouted Alberto and José like mad things.

'Defend yourself, you old wolf, your hour has finally come!'

And José:

'The German artillery trounces the French defences!'

The French defences – Pili and the Baby – were fiercely resisting being trounced when Helena suddenly cried out in the strangest of voices:

'Stop it! Get out of here!' and then she turned

on the light and started yelling for Aunt Honorina.

In normal circumstances, it was considered a great betrayal to summon grown-ups to protect you, but these were not normal circumstances.

Helena, grave-faced, was sitting on the edge of her ruined bed, her face scarlet, her narrowed eyes shining, and she was looking at us with a mixture of fear and hatred.

I was looking back at her and then all I could think of was to stare down at the floor and clumsily try to button up my pyjama jacket.

'What are you doing here?' asked Helena.

'What do you think? The same thing we do every year, we're here for the great Battle of Verdun. . .'

But no one knew any more what we were doing there, it was impossible to say why we were there. We couldn't understand how we'd ever come up with the idea of the great Battle of Verdun in the first place, why we'd ever even thought of it, when, to be honest, we'd never much enjoyed it, and which we'd never. . .oh, I don't know- . . .which had never. . .

Again the shadows intertwined on the ceiling. Aunt Honorina burst into the room like a Borneo waterspout, wiping her mouth with her napkin and waving her arms about.

'Oh, dear God, dear God!' she was screaming. 'Why, Lord, have you sent me this cross to bear?' and she looked so utterly ridiculous that Alberto and José couldn't keep a straight face.

I could though. I vaguely sensed that God really had sent her a cross to bear. And Helena must have sensed it too, because she was looking at me very seriously, as if we were all at mass, and she didn't say a word.

The carpet was covered in socks, dresses, hair ribbons, stuffing from the pillows and bits of lampstand.

Aunt Honorina was also looking at us in way she never had before and she gestured to us to get out.

We left, dumbstruck, half-surprised, half-sad, like Adam and Eve driven out of Eden, and without saying a word, we got back into our beds.

My bed was warm and rumpled like Helena's. I don't know why I knew that there would be no

47

punishments, not even any scoldings, and that no one would ever speak again of The Expedition, not the grown-ups, not Uncle Arturo, and probably not even Helena.

But I couldn't get to sleep. I kept tossing and turning, and the sheets came untucked first here, then there. And more than that. . .no, I can't explain it. . .

The bedroom ceiling was blue and very high and it was trembling. And it smelled of ether and sounded like a buzzing of bees, like in summer at siesta time. . .

But no, that's not it, no, I can't explain. . .

The light from the lighthouse came closer and closer and finally entered the room as if licking the wall where my bed and the sheets and the ceiling and the floor and my face were. And everything filled up with bright stripes of light. And once, suddenly, in the middle, but very high up, in the middle of a vast, blue vault, with really sad music playing. . . But, no, I'll never be able to explain what I mean. . . Yes, and Helena behind me, calling to me, naked and weeping, from a very dark, sad meadow. And Papa and Mama and Uncle

Arturo and Aunt Honorina, all of them leaning out of the lit windows of a train, saying goodbye, goodbye, to Helena and to me, as we walked naked through the snow, with not a single tree in sight, and a man at our backs, carrying a whip, and we knew that we'd never ever see them again. . .

And on and on like that for ever, with Helena talking to me, very softly, talking softly in my ear, as we walked through this strange country, so high and blue and full of those brilliant stripes of light, and suddenly everything vanished, as if it had simply dissolved, and we had to gather up the bright stripes that were almost blinding us and, far off, I could see Helena again, crying softly and stroking a little roe deer in a very broad, green meadow with lots of birds singing in the sky and some bright, very white waves, all running ahead of the wind, running ahead of the wind, eyes clouded with tears. . .

# II

# WINTER

1

## GOD'S JOY

We'd end up with cold feet and a hot head and be filled by a kind of drowsy feeling or else a sort of reddish veil would cover our eyes, and our mouths would grow dry and tremulous. But that wasn't the worst of it, far worse than that was the feeling of remorse. . .

The room was in darkness. The last glimmer of twilight was dissolving behind the rooftops, behind the trees in the school garden, behind a great solitude that was like a vast, bitter emptiness that kept growing, getting nearer and nearer, becoming ever more concave, and that would soon swallow us up like death. . . And it really was death, because we'd lost the grace of God, which was worse than losing life itself, because it meant being guilty all over again for the Passion and

Death of Our Lord, even though Jesus Christ had died for our salvation. And that really was an act of ingratitude, a terrible sin, worse than murdering your own mother or father, much worse, because, after all, they'd only given us temporary life, whereas Jesus Christ had given us eternal life. And sinning was like giving the Blood of Our Lord to the dogs to drink or even worse than that, worse than anything. And we didn't care at all about Hell, only the pain of our own ingratitude. And we used to think sometimes that we'd be happier in Hell, because then we'd know that God, quite rightly, was taking his revenge on us, and we, in turn, would be able to vent our anger on him and hate him back. You'd feel happier hating God than knowing he'd died for our love and that even though we loved him, we continued to sin and, in doing so, again placed on his head the crown of thorns and scourged him and gave him the heavy cross to carry and nailed him to the cross and raised him up on it; and the nails would once more tear horribly at his wounds as the cross was placed in the ground and as it lurched upright when it hit the bottom of the hole; and we would again offer him the sponge soaked in vinegar and hyssop, and pierce his side with a spear. And we were all silent and afraid, more afraid than sorrowful, because we were bad and deserved to be struck down by God and sent to Hell rather than back home for supper with Papa and Mama, who knew nothing about all this and who kissed us, unaware that they were kissing condemned men. And it made you squirm to kiss Mama, who was so soft and white and kind, and to touch her with the same lips that had kissed pictures of naked, disgusting, stinking women.

It was impossible to go on living in that state, knowing that each minute, each second lived in sin meant making Jesus relive his agony; and wherever you looked, at a wall, at the floor, up at the sky, you saw Jesus's sad, sad face, with those large, deep eyes and the crown of thorns on his head and the blood trickling down over his forehead and his face. And the blood flowed and flowed until it drenched the ground you walked on, and you could hardly move and you felt sticky all over. And as long as you were in that state of mortal sin, every day was grey, even if it was

55

sunny, and everything turned out wrong and the teacher always asked you the one bit of the lesson you hadn't revised, and Papa was in a bad mood and Mama was sad, and when you played football, no one passed the ball to you or, if they did, you missed one of the easiest passes ever, and, worse than that, whenever you were in a state of mortal sin, Sporting Gijón F.C lost even though they were playing at home or else they drew, which, when you're playing at home, is the same as losing. And it was really hard to explain why that should be, because you thought: 'Just because I've sinned doesn't mean God should punish everyone else who wants Sporting to win.' But this was one of the great mysteries it was best not to think about, like why did God create the world if He knew beforehand that Lucifer was going to rebel and that a lot of people would be damned for all eternity. And then, even if the Devil hadn't existed and there had been no original sin and we'd all lived happily ever after in the earthly Paradise, that still didn't explain why God created Adam and Paradise and the sea and the stars and everything. And then there were Adam and Eve's children who must have married their brothers and sisters, which is a mortal sin. And there were loads of other things like that.

But all of these questions arose from the fact that we humans couldn't really understand anything about what was really going on in the world, for example, we only saw the colours between red and blue, but there were many more, and then there was all that complicated stuff about vibration speeds and infrared and ultraviolet rays. And then, even though we could see the colours between red and blue, we could never be sure that other people saw them as we did, because if, for example, a person is told from birth that a particular colour is called green, but she sees it the same way as I see red, and she sees red the way I see green, we'll never in our entire life know that we mean different things when we talk about red or green. And if that's the case with simple things like colours, it must be even more complicated with other things. Besides, we can't necessarily trust our reason. Because, for example, if you take two convergent straight lines and make the gap between them as large as possible, they'll eventually meet at some ever more distant point, but they'll never be parallel, because you can't imagine a space big enough to ensure that those two straight lines will never ever meet, and you certainly couldn't imagine them diverging, but then, according to that argument, there must only be convergent lines in the world, which is nonsense. But that just goes to show that you can't trust reason and that the arguments put forward by Voltaireans and unbelievers aren't worth a bean, and we must be humble and recognise the limitations of human intelligence and submit ourselves to the authority of the Church, because that's the only way we'll get to Heaven and see God and, seeing God, understand all the incomprehensible things that used to torment us simply because we couldn't understand them, and when that happens, we will love and worship and feel God's power as never before.

But you couldn't think like that when you were in a state of mortal sin, because then the Devil filled you up with base thoughts, and you didn't want to go to Heaven and it felt like you couldn't be sure of anything, not even that God existed or that the Holy Virgin Mary existed and you felt alone and sad and wanted to spit at everything, at the priests and the churches too. But you couldn't live that way, because you felt a kind of tingle down your spine and a desire to vomit, and especially when everything was so sad and it was always raining and everything smelled of cough lozenges and there was nothing to look forward to; and Jesus's face was always there before you, and even though he said nothing, he was looking right inside you and with all that blood dripping down his face as well. And in the end, you had no choice but to go to the Father Confessor's room.

And the Father Confessor's room smelled of sweet soap and damp, and the Father Confessor would be writing in the light of a lamp with a green shade, and you could see his very soft, white hand writing very slowly, forming large, round letters, and there was a special pleasure in following his pen with your eyes and seeing how carefully he finished off each letter, and I don't know why, but you felt a kind of joy whenever he completed a word or a capital letter; but gradually you'd start to feel nervous because the Father Confessor wasn't saying anything and that hand was writing so slowly it seemed it would never stop, and you could hear the other day-pupils going home and the boarders filing into the dining room for supper, but, above all, you were aware of the image of Jesus looking down at you and becoming brighter and bigger, his eyes full of tears, and in the end, you couldn't resist that look and you'd throw yourself, weeping, at the feet of the Father Confessor, who would stop writing and stroke your head, saying: 'My child, my child,' and his cassock smelled the same as the room, only stronger and with just a whiff of mothballs.

And when you raised your head, you'd see the Father Confessor, and the smile on his face was fixed like the smile of a dead man, and his eyes were sad like Jesus's eyes, half-closed, looking at some point above your head. And the whole room was in darkness apart from the desk and a bit of the Father Confessor's left arm, and all you could hear was the tick-tock of the Father Confessor's clock which stood on the desk at the feet of a Christ carved out of yellowish ivory and hanging on a black cross just like the crucifixes you get on coffins. And you didn't have to say anything, you just cried and cried and that filled you with a kind of strange, inexplicable joy, but it was as if you were once more entering a large, brightly-lit house where Papa and Mama were waiting for you, and it was as if we were coming home from a dark, sad, cold, muddy land where we knew no one and where everyone hated us. And it seemed that the grace of God was like a hot shower that fell on us, washing our body clean of something sticky and viscous, making us feel lighter and able to see more clearly.

And then the Father Confessor would take you by the hand and lead you down to the chapel, which was empty and dark and smelled of sweat and the breath of those who had just left. And the Father Confessor would cover his face with his hands and bow his head and begin to say a prayer to the Blessed Sacrament which was there before us, with the dying red flame of a candle in front of it. And we prayed – 'Forgive me, Father, for I have sinned' and 'My Lord Jesus Christ'. And you could hardly pray at all because the words got muddled up and you felt like bursting into tears all over again and staying there for ever in the chapel so close to Jesus, who was so kind and so alone. And you wanted more than that: you wanted to be sent as a missionary to a tribe of Indian savages and to suffer hunger and exhaustion and despair, but all for Jesus's sake, and then to be sacrificed by the savages, with the drums beating all around and the Indians dancing, drunk and stark naked, and the women too. And then you'd suddenly realise that you were thinking about the naked women and that you were sinning all over again, but this time it was even worse because you were in chapel, with the Father Confessor praying beside you and the Sacrament right there in front of you, and that seemed so sinful you could barely think. But it wasn't really your fault, because you could never tell what you might think next, because the thoughts came along all connected up together, and there was no point trying to think of something else, because whatever you thought about, the Devil was always ready to slip in something sinful. And there was no point saying to yourself: 'I'm not going to think about anything' because you can't ever think about nothing, at the very least you can think that you don't want to think about anything, but then, there you are, thinking about something. And the only way you could get rid of evil thoughts was to imagine a woman sitting on the toilet doing her business and to concentrate on every detail until you felt the temptation had passed. But it was pretty disgusting to think about such things there in the chapel, and then what were you supposed to do, because the moment you relaxed, the Devil would slink in between the bars of your thoughts and you'd find yourself thinking about the posters advertising the Rio Carnival that you'd seen in sleeping cars, or the drawings from *What Every Young Man Should Know Before He Gets Married*, or Manassé's 'artistic' photographs, and you couldn't splice and solder thoughts together quickly enough to stop all those images surfacing. And praying a few Ave Marias, as we were told to do in the Spiritual Exercises, didn't really help because while you might start off thinking about the angel who came to tell the Virgin that she was going to be the Mother of God and carefully ponder each word he'd said, it was impossible to do the same with every Ave

Maria you prayed, you just couldn't, it was really boring thinking the same thing thirty or forty times and then it was as easy as anything for the Devil to prevail. And how you suffered, struggling and struggling against temptation, and sometimes you wondered if it wouldn't be better to die in grace right there and then and go directly up to Heaven where all that suffering would finally be over and the Devil would have no power. And at other times you wondered if there weren't some pills you could take, a kind of aspirin or paracetamol, to get rid of temptations. Besides, it felt like God was being most unfair, after all, it wasn't our fault we were born. Because being born was taking a gamble on whether we went to Hell or to Heaven and if we said, right, we'll bet on the danger of going to Hell against the probability of going to Heaven, then, fine, God would be perfectly within his rights to send us down to Hell if we lost, but not otherwise, because he was forcing us to take part in a game whether we wanted to or not and, anyway, it was hardly our fault if Adam and Eve sinned, I mean, we weren't there to tell them not to eat the apple. But thinking such

64

things was a sin too, because all the mysteries are much more complicated than you imagine, and when you think about it, we really don't know anything, and God alone knows what the real truth is.

Because probably inside just one molecule in my body there are many atoms and inside each atom there are electrons and protons and inside each electron and each proton there are other even smaller things and still more things inside those, and inside those are other worlds like ours, with sky and sea and boats and men and women and wars and religions and everything, well, they might not be exactly like our world, they'd be things we couldn't even imagine, but they'd be similar. And probably the world we live in is just a part of a part of a part of a part of a part of an electron of an atom of a molecule of a hair of some great giant or some other creature too strange even to imagine. And probably that giant or whatever is just a man who lives in a hut in a village in a corner of a province of a region of a state of a continent of a planet of a planetary system of a universe which is part of an electron of an atom or a molecule of the hair of another giant a trillion trillion times bigger and so on until you almost go mad thinking about it. Because it does send you mad thinking about these things, and even though you feel they're probably true, you can't quite believe it, because there can't be such big, extraordinary things, although who knows, for example, what flies think of men.

I mean if it ever occurred to a fly that it was perched on the shorts of a football player, and that soon the player would be coming to put them on in order to play a game in the first division of the Spanish League, and that there was another championship in England and another in Germany and another in Italy and so on in every major country in the world, the fly would think it all complete nonsense, and there would be many other things that would be impossible for a fly ever to imagine, like Newton's binomial theorum or the chemical formula of nicotine. And who knows how many other things there are that we know nothing about, even stranger things than the Holy Trinity, things that are probably going on right now and which we're part of, only we don't know it.

And it's as if time didn't exist at all and as if, at this very moment, Hernán Cortés was marching into Mexico or Moses was asking God to part the Red Sea or. . .and this really is amazing. . .yes, it's as if, at this very moment, Adam and Eve were eating the apple and, in some truly mysterious way, it's as if whenever I commit a sin, I'm eating the apple with them, and I myself – yes, I myself – am committing the original sin, and that's phenomenal, and you could even think that all the men who have existed or will exist in the world are Adam and all the women are Eve and that would explain why we're all responsible for original sin. . . But that was way too complicated, and it got to the point when you could barely think at all and it was sort of sweet and refreshing to hear Brother Hermida gently practising on the harmonium, which was at the back of the chapel where everything lay in darkness apart from a yellow lightbulb above the harmonium, and you could see Brother Hermida swaying very slowly and the music was always very high and full of tremolos, and it made you think of the Virgin descending on clouds with the Baby Jesus in her arms and smiling a really kind, really beautiful smile as if she was telling us that we were sure to go to Heaven. And you didn't know how to thank her for that smile and you wanted to fight and die for that poor, sweet, pretty Virgin. And you'd have been really pleased if suddenly everyone was pursuing and trying to kill the Virgin, and you were the only one left to defend her, and it was winter and you had to run away with her into a forest full of snow and hide away in a cave, just the two of you, and have all kinds of other adventures before your enemies found you and hurled themselves, screaming, on the Virgin, intending to kill her, and the Virgin just stayed there, kneeling on a bare hillside, praying, very still and very pale, and then you, as if naked and filled with rage, because they were many and the Virgin was a woman alone, and so good and so gentle too, turned on them, and somehow set about killing them all, which was simultaneously exciting and sickening, seeing blood spurt from their mouths, like bulls at the final kill, and seeing them stagger, again like bulls, and writing about and suffering and suffering some more and then dying very slowly until they could stand the pain no more; and even though you were covered in blood and your mouth tasted of salt, you took a fierce, furious pleasure in walking amongst the dying and sticking a stake through someone's eyes so that a kind of reddish-greenish goo spilled out and, if they screamed, driving the red-hot point of a sword through their throat or twisting their arms until the bones broke or else squeezing their head in a kind of press until, pop, it split like a hazelnut, and a great gush of blood poured from their ears and eyes and nose and mouth, and then they would put their arms around your legs, weeping and begging you not to torture them, not to kill them, but you'd carry on torturing and killing and warning them in advance about the new torments you were going to inflict and telling them that they were going to die only in order to suffer still more.

And all of a sudden you'd realise that your jaws were clenched so tight that your teeth were hurting and that your nails hurt from digging them into the back of the pew in front. And it seemed to you then that thinking was like having your head full of little creatures as small as bits of shot whizzing round and round faster and faster until they left smoking furrows inside your head and it was just unbearable, and the creatures flew round faster and faster, getting hotter and hotter, and you trembled all over because you were afraid of dying, especially in a state of mortal sin, which was the state you were in just then, and besides, there was Mama, who was so good to you, and Papa and everyone else at home, and besides, you wanted to see more things in life and make long journeys, especially to see the Pacific islands at night, with a big moon and an almost lilac-blue sky and a vast beach with white waves breaking on the sand, making the most beautiful sound, and the foam retreating ever more slowly, with bits of tree bark floating in it, coming right up as far as the foot of the coconut palms, and you lying nearby, breathing very slowly, on a patch of sweet-smelling grass, utterly alone and with the sound of ukeleles rising and falling in the background amongst the trees, all lit up by colourful oil lamps. And then, out of nowhere, a Hawaiian girl would appear, naked apart from a garland of huge white flowers, two white flowers in her hair on either side of her forehead, and her white, white teeth, and she was smiling and had a firm, glossy body, and then, without saying a word, not a word, but smiling all the while, she would lie down beside you, and you didn't do anything, just gently stroked her hair. And you'd be together for a long time, until it began to grow light, and there was such a feeling of joy, and all the birds would start to sing, and flocks of really big birds, like peacocks, would fly over, their brilliant feathers, blue or red or yellow, gleaming in the rays of the sun as it rose above the sea, and the light almost dazzled you. And then you lay there half-asleep, and felt the girl's warm arm and her hands cupping your face and then, coming nearer, her breath and her parted lips with their white teeth and, between them, her tremulous tongue. And for some reason you'd be filled then by a terrible sense of disgust at it all and you'd feel feverish and as if you were splashing about in a bath full of pitch, and you'd have a terrible longing just to run away. . .

Most of all, though, you felt the pain of your

own weakness, because you were incapable of ever resisting temptation and it was pointless praying or doing anything. And you felt totally despicable, like an ass or a pig or the very lowest of beasts. And you would clutch your head in your hands and cry, your eyes burning with rage at your own wretchedness, and then when that first fit had passed, you would weep, out of a deep sense of grief and sorrow, which gave you goosepimples, and if you put your hand to your chest, you'd realise that your heart was barely beating. It was a feeling of great sadness because God was so far away, because he didn't see us or hear us and didn't care whether or not we loved him nor that we were battling day and night against the Devil. A great cold shadow very slowly penetrated the soul, and you felt so alone and forgotten by God, as if you were just a thing: like a worm or a table or a cloud. And you had other thoughts too, thoughts too horrible to be written down, and you even reached the point where you hated God with all the fury of your soul and, mysteriously, at the same time, loved him even more, as if you hated him because you loved him.

And suddenly, just when you couldn't take any more, when you felt burning inside you the joy of surrendering to the Devil, and felt the impossible-to-explain pleasure of insulting, wounding and offending the one thing you loved with such a passion that you would unhesitatingly have given up your life for the certainty that he loved you, just at that moment, the Blessed Virgin Mary would descend into the very depths of your soul and say: 'God loves you.' And then the whole world changed and filled with happiness, and it was as if a great blue sky had opened up and it was one long sunny Sunday morning, an immense, eternal Sunday, bright with springtime, which cannot be described in words. And that's precisely what happened. My body and soul felt as if they were swollen with happiness and with a great feeling of peace and love for everything. And I would wish then that I had the courage to say to the Father Confessor who was still praying at my side how much I loved him and to Brother Hermida too, who was still softly playing the harmonium, and to all my friends and everyone at home and to all the people and all the animals and to everything that exists in the world.

And then a great time of happiness would begin.

When I went home for supper, I found my cousins, who had come for the match the following day, and everything was full of shouting and noise. Uncle Arturo and other friends of Papa had come as well, and all the men were sitting by the fire, smoking and drinking brandy and soda. They told me to join them and asked what I thought of the two line-ups – especially Sporting's line-up – and what my friends at school had to say about the form of the various players.

'Because I reckon,' said one of Papa's friends, 'that there isn't a place in Spain where they know more about football than in a Jesuit college.'

'And they've produced some really splendid players.'

And then they started listing all the good players who had been to Jesuit schools, and there were loads of them, especially in Bilbao Athletic F.C. I had never felt happier. It was the first time in my life that I'd taken a serious part in a conversation with the men, and it was so good to be with them, listening to them talking so slowly and confidently, only laughing at things that were genuinely funny, not jumping from one subject to another the way kids do and not all shouting at once and talking nonsense like the women! It was especially good to be there sitting next to Papa, watching the flames from the fire reflected on the glasses and on the bottles of brandy and soda, and the men smoking their cigarettes and blowing out blue smoke.

A friend of Papa's was there too, a manager with Sporting, and he asked me about an Argentinian friend of mine at school, Colubi, who was older than me, in year six, and was brilliant at football and about to try out for Sporting's youth team, and, if he did well, then, in two years' time, he could end up playing for the first team. I told him that in the next few days the school was due to play the Instituto and that Colubi would be in the team. Then the director said that he and the trainer would come to the match and would I mind introducing them to Colubi, because if they liked the way he played, they'd need to talk to him.

I was thrilled to be able to have a small part in Colubi possibly one day playing for Sporting and so I said, no, of course I wouldn't mind. I was positively aglow.

Then everyone started telling old football stories and about the amazing time my father and the others once had when they went to Santander to watch a play-off between the Asturian team and the Basque team, and how they got into an argument with some supporters from Bilbao and, after the match, offered them the chance to get even by playing a series of chess games on the train back to Bilbao, but the games continued all the way to San Sebastián, and, in the end, they only got off the train in Biarritz, without so much as a word to anyone at home about where they were going, and with no money to pay for a hotel.

And how they laughed to remember their adventures in Biarritz where they were mistaken for friends of the Prince of Wales, who was staying there at the time, and the party at the casino where my father and his friends climbed up onto the stage where the orchestra was playing and forced the musicians to stop so that they could sing instead. Everyone laughed to remember this, and then Uncle Arturo said: 'Wasn't this what we sang?' and with that, he got up from his armchair and, with a glass of brandy in his left hand and with his right hand pressed to his heart like an Italian tenor, he leaned forward and started singing very softly:

*Open the door, child, I'm frozen to the bone,*
*I'm the captain of a ship that has gone under. . .*

'Was it "Gone under" or "split asunder"?' asked Papa.

'We always said "gone under", said Uncle Arturo, 'that's what the maid taught me.'

'Oh, well, in that case,' said another man, 'there's no more to be said.'

'Who can remember what we sang after that?' asked Uncle Arturo.

'It was "Santos Dumont",' replied my father.

And suddenly, they all rose to their feet, glasses of brandy in one hand and the other pressed to their breast in imitation of Uncle Arturo, and sang:

*Santos Dumont invented a balloon*
*That could be driven on hot air only. . .*

I stood up to sing too, and Uncle Arturo said:
'This lad needs some fuel.'

And Papa smiled, and Uncle Arturo took a glass, poured me a brandy and soda and handed it to me with a bow, saying:

'Now you're a man.'

And then we all started singing together:

*Santos Dumont invented a balloon*
*That could be driven on hot air only. . .*

And at that point, Mama and Aunt Honorina came into the room and Mama said:

'Don't go giving the child brandy!'

'Come on, ladies too,' said Papa, and he almost dragooned Mama and Aunt Honorina into joining the choir and poured them each a brandy and soda.

'No, please,' protested the ladies. 'Stop, that's enough. It'll go to my head.'

But by then, Mama and Aunt Honorina had

started laughing, saying: 'You are a bunch of clowns!' and Papa put his arm around Mama's waist and Uncle Arturo did the same with Aunt Honorina, and the other men started booing and saying: 'That's not fair' and burst out laughing again. Then they all took up the song:

*While seated in his basket. . .*

At which point, Olvido the maid came in and said 'Supper's served,' and opened the door to the dining room.

And there we saw the table laid as if for a banquet, with the best crockery and the starched napkins and the candelabra with candles burning in them. And all the cousins – Alberto, José, Pili and the Baby – who had been having baths and washing their hands, came down to supper and started laughing at us and applauding.

'To get the full effect we need to turn out the lights,' said Uncle Arturo.

And Olvido, who was standing at the door, almost crying with laughter, half covering her face with her apron, turned out the lights. And then all you could see was the glow from the wood fire in the living-room and, beyond, in the dining room, the ten candles in the candelabra, five on each side of the table, and the glitter from the glasses and the cutlery and the plates and the vases of flowers.

'Ten out of ten for the ladies,' said one of the guests, and Mama replied:

'Oh, don't be taken in by appearances, it's only cheap stuff.'

'Art, Madam, has no price.'

And then I felt such joy inside me that my whole body trembled and, without knowing why, I laughed out loud. I felt full of the grace of God, at peace with God and with all the people I most loved, who were there, loving and happy, beside me, and I wished then that the world would stop, that time would stop and that one instant would last for ever. But that wasn't really what I wanted. Because tomorrow was sure to be an even happier day, even more crammed with happiness, and great things would doubtless happen, things you couldn't even dream of.

'Come on, off to Belshazzar's feast,' said Papa, and we all headed into the dining room.

Everyone was talking at once and laughing, and Uncle Arturo, as if he were the captain of the troops, went on ahead and started singing the rest of the song about Santos Dumont:

*Come back down to earth, Dumont,*
*The committee's here to see you. . .*

Then everyone else shaded their eyes with one hand as if gazing down from the basket of a hot-air balloon, and we all marched into the dining room, singing:

*The committee can do as it oughta*
*But I'm off to the Rock of Gibraltar.*

while the cousins shouted and applauded and laughed and laughed and laughed.

# III

# SUMMER AGAIN

1

## ONE MORNING

It was morning. We were driving along in a cart, and the cart smelled of dry grass and ripe apples.

The donkey was called Manolina and was grey. Grey.

We were going to the station to fetch the cousins arriving from Madrid for the summer.

The gardener, the owner of the cart, was called Manuel the Gardener and he looked after the garden, making sure that no weeds or grass appeared amongst the flowers.

Manuel the Gardener stank of wine and if ever we went to his house when he was having supper, he'd offer us some too, and when he picked up a glass, he'd hold it up to the light and say very seriously 'Christ's blood', and he always left smeary fingerprints on the glass and urged on the donkey with a very shiny hazel switch.

Some of the fields were full of dew and others were full of sunshine and poppies.

It smelled of May and blue sun.

Don Robustiano was passing on his bicycle, the pedals creaking. He always cycled to work because he was a Republican and a spiritualist and hadn't got married in church and had long, untidy grey hair like St John the Baptist and resembled the fakir and mind-reader Flormax.

When he overtook us, we shouted: 'Don Robustiano doing your rounds, just you wait till the last strumpet sounds!' And then we crossed ourselves and sang the national anthem.

At home they told us that it wasn't 'strumpet' but 'trumpet', but it was much funnier to say 'strumpet', which means 'a loose woman'.

Because it was windy, Don Robustiano couldn't quite hear us and so he waved as he passed, smiling and raising one hand from the handlebars, and because he wasn't very good at riding a bike, he lost control and fell off right in front of the cart.

Then he got up, pretending to laugh, and dusted off his knees the way the men did at mass after the Elevation.

'I'm too old for this kind of thing,' he said to Manuel and looked at us rather sadly.

That would have been the perfect moment, now that he could hear us properly, to repeat what we'd said about the 'last strumpet', but we couldn't bring ourselves to do so even though we knew it was a mortal sin to think that an atheist like Don Robustiano could possibly be a good man, and we felt almost sorry for him and felt bad about being so rude to him when he was bound to end up in Hell.

The gust of wind from the sea made the canvas awning on the cart flap and crack.

We clattered into Gijón, bouncing up and down in the cart.

The streets of Gijón were full of cool, clean, lilac-coloured shade and there was almost no one around, because these were the morning streets filled by the smell of seaweed.

A water wagon was passing by, in the form of a pearl-grey truck whose tyres smelled of wet rubber, and we shouted to the men to spray some water on us too and cool off Manolina, who was sweating, and wash the dust off the cart.

They took no notice of us and drove on, grave-faced.

The driver had a black moustache and was smoking a barely-lit cigarette.

When we reached the station, the train was already in and our cousins were there, along with Helena, who looked very pale and serious and sad. I smiled at her, but she didn't respond.

The grown-ups, who had arrived there earlier in the car, were all talking at once, kissing everyone, left, right and centre.

Aunt Honorina, like a crazed chicken, screeched in a tearful, clucking voice as if she could barely speak:

'Just look at the state of these poor children!'

But it really wasn't that bad.

One of the station staff, whose name was Belarmino and who looked as if his name was Belarmino because he was fat and spoke very slowly and had a red face and wore a nankeen jacket with a bottle of milk sticking out of one pocket, said:

'You have to bring up little 'uns as if they were goats,' and then he beamed, but Aunt Honorina and the other ladies glared at him, and he fell silent and went away.

'Who asked him to stick his nose in?' asked one lady. But no one knew, because no one *had* asked him.

A stranger newly arrived from Madrid said that it was all the rage in Germany and the United States to give children their independence.

The ladies started discussing which children should go to which houses and in which cars. We children wanted to go in the Overland touring car because it was faster than Uncle Arturo's poor old jalopy.

The stranger declared that 'Abroad', mothers left their little nippers in a cage all day.

'Yes, so that they can go off and enjoy themselves,' retorted the ladies with a sardonic smile. 'We don't want any of that "Modern" stuff here, thank you very much.'

And with that, they started kissing us.

The modern gentleman backed off and went to help Uncle Arturo start the jalopy, which cleared its throat, but did not immediately spring into life.

'So how would they get this car started in Germany or the United States, then?' Uncle Arturo enquired of the modern gentleman, and everyone laughed, especially the ladies.

'But you, I see, have had your hair cut short,' said the modernist to the ladies.

We all looked at Aunt Honorina, who had indeed had her hair cut in Paris *à la garçonne*. Cutting your hair *à la garçonne* was 'Modern', and Aunt Honorina took immediate offence at this remark because she had been told by a lady from the Catholic Conference that the Pope had excommunicated 'Modernism'.

Uncle Arturo chuckled to himself, but when he caught Aunt Honorina's eye, immediately put on a very serious face, and the girls who, apart from Helena, were all extremely silly, started whispering and giggling in the 'Overland' where they were sitting, jigging up and down on the seats in their excitement.

The ladies, seething with rage, started slapping them, but no one cried, knowing that this was precisely what the ladies wanted.

Belarmino emerged again from the Station Master's office with his greenish bottle of milk in his pocket and said very prissily as he passed:

'I hope you have a most pleasant summer season,' and everyone burst out laughing and he looked at us, most put out.

Fortunately, at that point, Uncle Arturo went over to him and asked him to turn the starting handle while he pumped the accelerator pedal. Milk-guzzling Belarmino gradually began to smile until his face was like a bright moon, and when the car finally started, he looked at us, very pleased and smug, while he wiped his hands on a filthy piece of cotton cloth which he produced from his trouser pocket.

Uncle Arturo's jalopy was shaking like a wet dog, and from inside, Uncle Arturo asked:

'Isn't anyone coming with me?'

We all felt sorry for Uncle Arturo because he wasn't a real grown-up and he played with us and defended us and we wanted to go with him in his shaky old jalopy, and the girls all tumbled, shouting and shoving, out of the 'Overland' and into his car. The Ladies, most put out to have been left alone, sat muttering like pouter pigeons:

'Faddish creatures!'

But they just had to lump it and go on their own.

The jalopy set off, and we left the ladies gesticulating furiously amidst a cloud of bluish smoke the way cockroaches do as they lie dying in a puff of insecticide spray.

See you never, ladies! But the ladies had climbed into the 'Overland' and, driven by Saturnino, my grandfather's chauffeur, they were getting ever closer.

It was a thrilling drive.

Racing along in the wind, we passed through spots of yellow sun, through areas of paler sunlight, through streets of cool, blue shade, through hot, grey shade, through the smell of seaweed, the smell of pines, the smell of car grease, along the street of the woman who owned dogs and always wore a spotted dressing-gown, past the balcony of the shop assistant who sang opera in the mornings with the doors flung open while he tied his tie, through the winter places which, in summer, were so very different.

Helena sat in front, next to Uncle Arturo, not saying a word. She looked very serious, very grown-up. Now and then Uncle Arturo would glance at her and smile. I wanted to talk to her, but the words wouldn't leave my throat.

Uncle Arturo whistled as he drove, and now and then he deliberately swerved so as to frighten the ladies in the car behind.

Otherwise, Uncle Arturo whistled as he drove, and sang:

> *The sun has ceased to shine*
> *Since you left the old town. . .*

beating time on the door.

When he made a particularly thrilling swerve, we all clapped and screamed, and people stared at us in amazement. I wished the pavements could have been full of ladies in black, wearing

93

gold-rimmed spectacles so that I could have spat at them to right and left and my spit would have hit them right slap bang on the lenses of their glasses.

The quay was full of seagulls. The masts and the ropes on the boats gleamed white, red and green in the golden sunlight. A cool, cheerful breeze was blowing. The sky was blue, blue. The stevedores next to the cranes shouted to one another. A boat painted bright red was leaving the harbour, sounding its siren.

Goodbye! It was the ladies overtaking us. Uncle Arturo smiled mysteriously. We let the ladies enjoy their triumph. Now was the moment, now that there was no one keeping watch on us from behind. Leaving Gijón, we turned right and drove to a cider bar amongst the trees.

We sat down and Uncle Arturo ordered two bottles of cider. One for him and the other for us.

We were sitting at a table outside, underneath some oak trees.

Uncle Arturo poured the cider really well, holding the bottle high above the glasses, and it was lovely to hear it fizzing into the glass and to see the golden yellow stream glittering as the sun caught it, and to see the dark green bottle growing gradually paler and more transparent.

Helena sat down beside me and I grasped her hand under the table. She let me hold her hand, and she smiled. And I was happy, so happy I could have burst with pleasure.

At the next table, four fat men with red faces were drinking cider and eating spider crabs.

'They're not all yours, are they?' they asked Uncle Arturo.

'No, they're my nieces and nephews.'

The men laughed and said how pretty Helena was, and she was pleased.

They came over and offered us some spider crabs in their dirty, greasy hands. Helena huddled closer to Uncle Arturo and squeezed my hand harder.

The four men stood in front of us, then crouched down a little, put their heads together and started to sing. They sang, and very well too, a sad, very pretty song:

*If your good father was still here*
*You'd wear necklaces of silver,*
*But not now, my child, not now,*
*Not now, my child, not now. . .*

Uncle Arturo was listening intently, and I saw that Helena had tears in her eyes and pressed closer to Uncle Arturo as if she were afraid. The singers opened and closed their mouths, breathed in and breathed out, as seriously as if they were praying, their gaze lost as if they were looking deep inside themselves. And one of them was still holding a bottle of cider in his hand, and the bottle was trembling. Their voices grew suddenly louder:

*Not now, my child, not now. . .*

and then gradually softer, very sad, very sweet.

The oak trees cast a greenish shade and spots of sunlight moved across the ground and over the tables. At the door of the bar, a dog was sleepily scratching itself, its eyes drowsy and red. The day was beginning to grow hot, and wasps and bright flies came buzzing by. Further off, between the trees, you could see green fields, villagers working amongst the maize, pale blue carts, oxen and a scrap of sea. The smell of damp grass warmed by the midday sun wafted to us on the air, and I, dying of happiness, with Helena by my side, half-closed my eyes and plunged deep into my thoughts. I was thinking about the summer that awaited me by Helena's side, beneath that sky, amongst the rivers and trees and green fields, knowing that she loved me, and my eyes almost filled with tears.

## 2

## IN THE WOODS

Of course I collect butterflies. It was the only one of my hobbies that my family encouraged.

The seamstress made me a net and, every Sunday, the grown-ups admired my collection. Sometimes, too, when conversation flagged, Aunt Honorina would remind her female visitors that I was, basically, an orderly child. Then, fearful that she had gone too far, she would temper this praise, saying:

'Well, when he wants to be.'

And the visitors all answered in glum agreement:

'Like all men.'

That morning, the meadows growing green by the river were singing in the sunshine. Barechested, I walked down the rough path towards the great hunting-place of berries and poppies. Helena, her long hair loose, walked beside me, on sweet and constant alert.

'Look!' she would shout. 'There's one!'

And I would plunge in among the bushes, scratching my arms in the process, and usually returning with nothing.

Helena became positively infuriating then and kept teasing me and repeating, quite falsely now:

'There's one!'

Like an idiot, I would race off in that direction, and she would burst out laughing again.

'Fooled you!'

Then, around mid-morning, by which time I'd have caught maybe three *Vanessas*, an extremely common *Pieris*, and a *Papilio machaon lithographicus*, Helena would escape into the woods.

The grass was too high for me ever to spot her. She knew this and guided me by her calls.

Guided me and provoked me. My legs were all scratched by thistles, my net had holes in it, my throat was dry, my voice hoarse. I'd shout:

'Helena, where are you?'

And from some extraordinarily distant place, she would answer:

'Over here!'

Until, at last, I found her in the wood, sitting on the grass. There was a gentle murmur of insects amongst the reeds, and Helena was right in the midst of them, smoothing her dress. Then she began to laugh. She laughed easily, for no reason, but it was highly infectious. I lay down beside her, annoyed by that spontaneous laughter, and yet despite my scratched legs, I laughed too. Helena stretched out her bare arms on the cool grass and, with her head resting on my chest, she talked to me about the clouds and about my heart.

'Your heart's beating so fast,' she said, 'I'm afraid it might suddenly leap out of your chest.'

I maintained a proud silence, as if to say: 'It might well do that.' Then Helena would talk to me about the clouds.

'That big one over there looks just like Africa. . .'

I would say indignantly:

'Since when has the Union of South Africa

ended in a point like that? That cloud could, at best, be South America.'

She wouldn't give up. It was her turn to attack me:

'You're not much good at geography, are you? Do you mean to say that the lump sticking out on the left is Peru?'

She was right. The lump was much more like Senegal or Rio de Oro... Although, even if we accepted, as the lesser of two evils, that narrow version of the Union of South Africa, there was still the problem of the missing island of Madagascar.

I pointed this out to Helena, and Helena looked desperately up at the sky. It was true, Madagascar was far too large an object to be omitted from any map of Africa.

Then Helena let out a yelp of triumph, and I felt as if the gods had declared war on me.

Madagascar, with its exports of coffee, vanilla and spices, was travelling across the sky from the east. Helena was laughing, and quite right too; I said nothing, and... But – O gods! – Madagascar was already having a joke at our expense. It reached its allotted place, then glided onwards. Now it was a peninsula of Mozambique, now it had passed right over, now a very transparent Madagascar was flying like Fergusson's hot-air balloon over the source of the Nile, it was crossing the south of the Congo, it had reached Angola and headed out into the Atlantic where it vanished en route to Rio de Janeiro.

Helena should have been embarrassed, she should have at least kept quiet. But, foolish girl, she laughed, and I was the one to feel embarrassed.

Then she consoled me and, out of respect for my wounded pride, said nothing... Far off, Madagascar was dissolving, and now the peninsula of Malacca was hoving into view.

The peninsula of Malacca was a most amusing piece of geography. It looked like the head and neck of some prehistoric animal sniffing the piece of meat that is the island of Singapore. And as if that wasn't enough, the cloud was remarkably white and insubstantial. The breeze driving it along stirred the tops of the tall trees, and the leaves murmured their contentment.

The green and gold light lent a ghostly air to everything. . . Poor Virgil! I had started translating Virgil that winter, and thanks to my teacher's ineptitude and my own lack of interest, I had made no progress at all. But I could see he was a good poet. That's why the wood reminded me of him.

> *Fortunate senex! Hic inter flumina nota*
> *Et fontis sacros frigus captabis opacum. . .*

What did it mean? Who knows, but whatever it meant, it was lovely. In the sleepy three o'clock class, I had enjoyed those *fontis sacros* and, above all, the surprising and delicious word *frigus* in the midst of the sultry hum of voices and flies. I didn't know what *frigus* was, but even so, I found it refreshing. . . *Frigus!* It didn't mean 'cold' or 'cool' or any of the other definitions in the dictionary; it was *frigus. Frigus, i* plus *u*, that cooling leap from *i* to *u*, with no intervening syllable, completely alone amongst all those overheated desks and the botflies buzzing at the windows. And then that final *s* like a fountain at the edge of the ice, like the preparatory noise we make before eating an ice-cream. The woods, of course, were *frigus*. 'Refreshing' was too long and 'cool' not expressive enough. It would be cool later on, but not yet. There was still dew on the nettles and on the north-facing gullies. The dry leaves still sounded like frost. Yes, *frigus* was the ideal word.

But how long have I been ignoring you, Helena? It must have been quite a while because you look ever so slightly sulky. Why so distant, Helena? Oh, there's no understanding girls. Helena was lying down on the green grass and appeared not to want to look at me. I went over to her and she, leaping like a cat, tried to escape. But I grabbed her again and, holding her spreadeagled on the ground, forced her to laugh and to cry. Why so angry, Helena? Aren't I allowed to think about Virgil without your permission? Really, it's too much! She, showing great astuteness, bit me on the shoulder and, taking advantage of my pain, quickly made her escape.

Fine, let her. I'll go back to Virgil.

*Hinc tibi, quae semper, vicino ab limite saepes*
*Hyblaeis apibus florem depasta salicti*
*Saepe levi somnum suadebit inire susurro. . .*

What did it mean? What did it matter? Did one need to know Latin in order to fall asleep sweetly to that *inire susurro*? How broad and deep the woods were! It made you feel like spending your entire life lying stretched out and naked, and letting everything happen somewhere else far away. . . Oh, I'm so stupid! Helena, where are you? You replied only with a distant: 'Yoohoo!' Where are you? The cuckoo's making fun of me too. Stupid Virgil! What's more my wound's bleeding, and it's all your fault, entirely your fault! What are you laughing at, Helena? I'm tired of this, where are you hiding?

'Here, I'm up here!'

'Up here' didn't tell me very much either.

'Where are you, Helena?'

The whole morning smiled among the ceaselessly trembling leaves, flickering on and off a thousand times per second like lights. In the fields down below, the villagers were calling to the oxen who responded by mooing almost rebelliously.

'Where are you?'

'Up here, in Chanito's pine tree!'

There was no doubt now. Leaping over roots and over rotting tree trunks, I ran, panting, up the slope. The air was full of infinitesimally thin strands of cobweb that I had to keep brushing away from my face. And yet, despite everything, the woods were enchanting. In the rays of light that slipped through among the oak trees, legions of brilliant insects, blue and green, rose and fell. . .

Ow! A low branch scraped the wound on my shoulder. The pain reminded me of the original offence and, renewing in me the desire to give Helena a good thrashing, made me walk still faster.

At last I saw her and, running towards her, I angrily threatened her with revenge. Now she had no escape! A tall nettle patch bristled behind her and I stood before her. But – were those real tears or merely pretend? – Helena was crying again and came limping over to me.

'What happened? Did you fall?' I asked.

But she didn't answer. She had noticed my wound and, wetting her handkerchief with spit, started to clean it. Meanwhile, with a kind of magnificent innocence, she told me off for my savagery.

'You boys are nothing but barbarians,' she said with a comically professorial air, 'complete barbarians.'

Naturally, the answer was simple enough. I merely had to ask who had inflicted the wound. But now that I thought about it, was I absolutely sure it had been Helena? Couldn't that stupid branch have been to blame? No, I couldn't accuse Helena just like that. She had enough to do cleaning my wound without me blaming her for ills she hadn't caused.

She – for she was a kind girl – was not so sure of her innocence. Once she had cleaned the wound, she apologised and showed me the small scratch on her leg. I had no alternative but to apologise as well and to lie down beside her on the moss.

Time moves very slowly when you're lying next to a girl! Especially if she's a girl like Helena.

Because Helena could speak without opening her mouth and be horribly provocative when she smiled that unbearable half-smile. In the end, she provoked me so much that I held her down by her arms and started kissing her. After the fifth kiss she wriggled free and ran down into the valley and the fields of poppies, shouting:

'This is one butterfly you're not going to catch!'

And I ran after her, shouting too, with the seamstress's improvised butterfly net fluttering joyfully in the wind.

Because, of course, I collect butterflies.

## 3

## AFTERNOON AND TWILIGHT

Opposite the empty fireplace, the grown-ups were drinking black coffee and golden liqueurs. The fireplace still smelled of the wood fires of winter, but it was summer now and because of the heat, the dining room lay in the half-darkness. The shutters were pushed to, but the sun's rays poured in, crowded with tiny shining motes that rose and fell. The conversation, spoken in the softest of tones, sounded very distant and gentle, as if a group of monks were praying in the choir and I were listening to them from the nave of an empty cathedral. A new, more brilliant ray of sun entered, causing Aunt Honorina's violet beads and the glasses of the gentleman visitor to glitter. It was hot, and the heat was like music and smelled of yellow candles. The servants came in to clear the table. Amongst the men's cigar smoke, the cutlery tinkled like the bells on a herd of goats grazing lazily in the noontide heat haze. It was siesta time, all soft and warm, all stretching and yawning, drowsing in the shade of a blue wood, in a deep dark land, in an age before Christ. The dining room lay in shadow and from the darkness you could hear the cicadas and the crickets singing in the sun and the sun purring over the greenish-yellow fields and the cool, cool clamour of the oak trees caught by a gust of salty, blue breeze from the sea.

Then I could resist no longer and I escaped to my room: I got undressed, pulled on my bathing trunks and raced out of the kitchen door. I ran down the hill, with the wind in my mouth, and Helena was waiting for me at the garden gate, wearing her red-and-gold-flowered swimsuit and her broad, yellow straw hat, and looking very happy and full of love and life, with her fair hair full of sunlight; and poking out of a hole in her canvas shoes was one big toe, which wriggled like a little mouse and made me feel like biting it and biting it for the rest of my life.

'Hi!'

'Hi!'

And we set off together, full of love, towards the great lands of the Afternoon. The sun – the Sun! – was snoring above the apple trees, and the fields were full of patches of sunlight. And there were woods of blue-black eucalyptus trees. And we felt a strange fear of those trees which were the trees of deathly pale madmen who walked about in white shirts and carried a knife dripping blood. They were the trees of tubercular women who spat blood, who had sunken chests and shining eyes filled with hate and who, when the sky was red at evening, howled like sad, hungry wolves and ran off with their mouths full of foam, grasping in one hand a very long, shiny, black needle so as to inject other people with their deadly poison. And beneath those trees there was always a poor toothless man chewing on a piece of bread.

The afternoon light was dense and golden and blue and black, a mysteriously terrifying light descending from the vast, lonely sky. A kind of torpor lay across the fields, a hot mist of cicadas and crickets, and way up high a kite was gliding.

113

Helena and I walked along in silence. Now and then, she stopped to pick a few blackberries and gave me half of what she picked. A few, those that had been in the sun, were warm, their skins dull; those that had been in the shade, were cold and bright. Sometimes, I was the one to pick them and give them to Helena, and we would eat them together, gazing into each other's eyes, our faces stained with the purple juice. And we continued walking, very close together, not saying a word, but trembling. My love, Helena - so beautiful with her brown skin and fair hair and blue eyes, so free and so brave – would stop again to pick blackberries and sometimes prick one of her fingers on a thorn. Then she would offer me her bloodied finger and I would suck the blood, so red, so salty, so beautiful, glittering in the sun. Then she would kiss me and wash away with her lips any blood that was still on mine. And then we would be filled by a strange fear. Because that was a secret ritual, a very secret ritual, like a kind of sin, although no one knew why. Helena pressed against me like a mysterious cat and with tear-filled eyes murmured: 'I'm afraid.' And I, full of tenderness and a love that made my eyes almost fill with tears, drew her closer to me and held her like that for a long, long time, until Helena lifted her head from my chest and looked up at me, still with tears in her eyes, but smiling now with love and happiness. Then we would walk on, our arms about each other, Helena resting her head on my shoulder. And on we would go, down to the sea.

The beach we went to in the afternoon was small and inaccessible. It was surrounded by very high cliffs, covered in some parts by nettles and ivy. Up above, the tops of the pine trees swayed about, silhouetted against the sky. As soon as we reached the sand, we took off our canvas shoes and hurled ourselves into the first foaming wave that came to meet us. Then we scrambled out again and put our shoes on a rock so that they wouldn't get buried in sand, and again we ran and flung ourselves into a cold, white, bubbling wave, so beautiful, so delicious, so furiously joyful that it made one mad with happiness. And sometimes I would somersault into the waves, something which I knew Helena liked me to do, even though she begged me not to, because someone or other –

a Frenchman I think – had broken his spine doing exactly that. And Helena would leave the water again, shrieking with joy, all smeared with sand and seaweed, red and yellow and green, all smelling of salt, her hair almost black now and straight, but looking even more beautiful than ever, her body wet and shining. And she would leap on me like a panther and push me under so that I swallowed water and then she'd run away until I caught her, climbed on top of her and pressed her head into the sand until her face and hair were well and truly coated and she, almost crying, would beg for mercy, and I – magnanimous Senatus Populusque Romanus – would let her have her freedom.

Then we would go back into the water and swim slowly along together, following the celebrated Hannon's Way, which involved swimming out to the Camel – a camel-shaped rock surrounded by a beard of foam – lying there on our backs for a while to take the sun, and afterwards plunging into a small, very clear, green pool that formed at high tide between the camel's two humps. And then we would swim on through a reddish, seaweed-clogged channel to reach the great, gloomy Rocks of Dr Frankenstein, where occasionally you could hear Echo, a sad creature imprisoned somewhere or other, who filled you with pity and who sometimes wept very quietly, very quietly. The great Rocks of Dr Frankenstein hurt your feet, and crabs hid in the caves there, and, once, we found a dead dog, its body all swollen and its mouth full of green flies. Among the great Rocks of Dr Frankenstein were very cold grottoes filled with a tremulous light, half-green, half-blue, and further in were the Roman Ruins with their great treasures and their mystery, with statues of pagan gods, white and naked, which would smile at Helena and me, and then, through another much narrower, far more spacious grotto, we entered the Ancient Time which existed there, at that very moment, with a bluer sky and a bluer, almost purple sea, and with an intensely blue breeze blowing and white birds that flew about singing. And you emerged into another even stranger world, full of a beauty you can't even think of without your heart stopping. Because the sun was setting and the sky was red and gold and the sea the colour of wine and there wasn't a breath of wind and it smelled of rosemary, roses and jasmine. . .

Helena was naked and tending a herd of goats. She was sitting by the sea, in a very green field that reached down to the water, beneath a tall laurel bush with very green, shiny leaves that glinted red in the golden light of the sinking sun. I was naked too and was coming ashore in a boat with golden sails, because I was a pirate captain born in Syracuse in Sicily, who had braved the dangers of thirst, hunger, heat and cold and all the other calamities of war and travel, and who had shown incredible powers of endurance. And I jumped from the boat into the water and swam over to the green meadow and started chasing Helena. But Helena ran faster than me and disappeared amongst the trees.

Then a man came by carrying a scythe on his shoulder and singing.

'The beautiful shepherdess you are seeking, young man, is the daughter of Aristoteles, he of the venerable words,' he said.

'Ancient and beautiful is the Hellenic language,' I replied, because that was the only example of Greek grammar I could remember.

The man with the scythe ran on ahead and led me to his house, where he offered me a frugal supper and, after dressing me in ragged peasant clothes and having placed the scythe on my shoulder, he said:

'Now, on behalf of Philemon the poor, go yourself to Aristotle, he of the venerable words, and tell him that you are the youth who I send to him as a servant. I, meanwhile, to the immortal gods, and especially to that goddess who over sweet and burning love presides, will make a sacrifice for your good fortune.'

And saying this, he indicated to me the road into the city.

He of the venerable words his house I discovered at last and he, seeing me, said:

'Praised one thousand and a thousand times more be the immortal gods, for without a doubt you are the youth who as a diligent servant my friend Philemon the poor has sent to me.'

He of the venerable words received me with

119

love and informed me of my obligations, for far was he from knowing my secret designs.

The brilliant twins (Castor and Pollux) were already hiding their light behind the dark horizon when I, believing the old man quiet and asleep, took off my poor rags and going into the room of my beloved, found her sleeping. Transported by joy and contentment and to the ever powerful goddess of love a thousand thanks giving, I carefully drew back the sheet that covered her and in the white light of the moon long did I contemplate the beauty of her body.

I kissed her then gently, so that little by little and in love she would wake, and she then, half-opening her eyes, said:

'There is no doubt but that Aphrodite has brought me this beautiful dream, for I feel by my side the young man whom I love.'

This said, she began with ardour to repay my caresses and kisses.

I did not want to let my mouth utter a single word, for I feared that thus the illusion of the dream would vanish and that she would dismiss me if she came too abruptly to her senses.

I enjoyed, then, in silence what in silence should be enjoyed, and when the cockerels began to crow I returned to the rustic bed that had been prepared for me in the stable for the servant I was.

Phoebus, father of love, pleasure and life, was already in the middle of his journey when I was woken by the angry shouts of Aristotle, he of the venerable words, saying:

'May the immortal gods bless me, but I have a queen and a king as servants.'

I jumped out of bed, bowed to my master and blamed the heaviness of my sleep on my weariness after the long journey and on many other reasons that my quick mind invented as I spoke.

I was just beginning to divert my master from his first intention, which was to dismiss me from his service (for the thought of leaving my lovely friend saddened me), when she entered with tears in her eyes and, prostrating herself at the feet of the old man, she said these or similar words:

'Forgive, good master, my idleness, but Aphrodite sent me such a dream this night that it is a miracle I can get up at all.'

The old man stood for a moment unmoving,

staring at her, and then, turning to me, he burst out laughing.

Helena and I gazed at each other in amazement, and the old man, taking us by the hand, drew us to him and said:

'Know this, young man, that she whom you possessed this night is not a poor rustic whom I employed as a servant (as she herself believes) but the daughter and heir of the Emperor of Athens. . .'

Helena was crouching in front of me, looking very serious and staring at me hard.

'What are you thinking about with those big wide eyes of yours?'

There she was, so fair, so beautiful, with her gleaming skin, her provocative blue eyes, that I could resist no longer and I leapt at her like a fierce Bengal tiger. She, however, jumped into the water first and I went after her and we started to swim and chase and splash each other. And we left the shadow of the rocks, where the water was dark and cold, and swam out into the sun, where the water was green and brilliant and warmer too, and it was a delight to dive down and to see Helena come to the surface, shaking her wet hair from her face and then plunging in again to explore the underwater channels thick with seaweed.

We walked contentedly up the beach and lay down in the sun. The sun was turning orange and sinking now behind the pine trees on the clifftop. The sky was green and full of a dark glow which, when you looked at it hard, was like Infinity. Sometimes a flock of birds would pass. Helena leaned her head on my shoulder and started making patterns on my skin with a little tickling trail of sand. And she kept looking and looking at me.

We walked back slowly, keeping very close, drunk on plenitude, pleasure and a strange, unbearable happiness, drunk on love, mad with love. My heart filled my whole chest, swelled my whole body with warm blood, filled my mouth with salt, filled the world with fierce joy, with passion, with colours as sharp as knives and at the same time as soft as the petals of a poppy, as honey, as milk straight from the cow. Trembling, in a hoarse voice, in a voice not mine, which came from who knows where, I said:

'Helena. . .I love you.'

And Helena, perfectly serene, grave-faced and beautiful, still gazing into my eyes, let herself be drawn closer, and when our lips were almost touching, she said:

'And I love you even more.'

And I drank in the breath of those words; I didn't hear them, I drank them in, breathed them in.

We said nothing more. We were walking along together, alone, through the silence of the evening. We were walking along alone through the silence of the world. Alone through the silence of time. Alone for ever. Together and alone, walking along together and alone through the silence of the world and the sea and the world, walking and walking. And everything was like a great archway through which we were passing and on the other side lay our world and our time and our sun and our light and our night and stars and hills and birds and always. . .

**Dedalus Euro Shorts**

Dedalus Euro Shorts is a new series. Short European fiction which can be read cover to cover on Euro Star or on a short flight.

*Titles include:*

*Helena* – Ayesta £6.99
*An Afternoon with Rock Hudson* – Deambrosis £6.99
*Alice, the Sausage* – Jabes £6.99
*Lobster* – Lecasble £6.99
*The Staff Room* – Orths £6.99
*On the Run* – Prinz £6.99

These can be bought from your local bookshop or online from amazon.co.uk or direct from Dedalus, either online or by post.. Please write to **Cash Sales, Dedalus Limited, 24–26, St Judith's Lane, Sawtry, Cambs, PE28 5XE**. For further details of the Dedalus list please go to our website www.dedalusbooks.com or write to us for a catalogue.

**The River** – *Rafael Sanchez Ferlosio*

"Taking place on a single sweltering August Sunday, Sanchez Ferlosio's excellent 1955 novel reads almost like a script, so privileged a position does it accord dialogue. By way of a welter of largely innocuous and inconsequential conversations between villagers and Madrilenos come to relax by the water's edge, the author achieves a nonetheless utterly captivating realism even as he subtly introduces symbolist intimations of Civil War battles and death stalking the land."

Chris Power in *The Times*

"The son of the Francoist intellectual Rafael Sanchez Mazas (the dandyist anti-hero of Javier Cerca's great *Soldier of Salamist*), Sanchez Ferlosio was still in his twenties when, in 1955, he wrote this remarkable landmark of Spanish realist fiction. Like some dappled Impressionist canvas, but with grimmer undertones, the novel sends a pack of day-trippers from stifling Madrid out into the country, to chat, flirt, dream and remember by the Jarama. A dialogue-driven portrait of Spaniards at play, *The River* – published with Franco's tyranny still in full spate – also acts as a sly political fable, as the Jarama (site of a bloody Civil War battle) slowly yields its secrets."

Boyd Tonkin in *The Independent*

"If I were to be asked one name, only one, from the Spanish post-war generation of writers, with the greatest possibilities of survival, that is to say, with standards of literary immortality, I would say, without a shadow of doubt, the name of Rafael Sanchez Ferlosio."

Miguel Delibes

**£9.99    ISBN 978 1 903517 17 8    406p    B.Format**